Penny
AND HER SONG

KEVIN HENKES

SCHOLASTIC INC.

Copyright © 2012 by Kevin Henkes.
All rights reserved. Published by Scholastic Inc., 557 Broadway, New York, NY 10012, by arrangement with Greenwillow Books, an imprint of HarperCollins Publishers. I Can Read Book® is a trademark of HarperCollins Publishers Inc. SCHOLASTIC and associated logos are trademarks and/or registered trademarks of Scholastic Inc.

10 9 8 7 6 5 4 3 2 1   18 19 20/0

Printed in the U.S.A.   40

Watercolor paints and a black pen were used to prepare the full-color art.
The text type is Century Schoolbook.

For Penryth

Chapter 1

Penny came home from school
with a song.

"Listen, Mama," said Penny.

"It's my very own song."

Penny started to sing,

"One is nice—"

"Your song is beautiful," said Mama,

"but you will wake up the babies."

So Penny looked for Papa.

"Listen, Papa," said Penny.

"It's my very own song."

Penny started to sing,

"One is nice, two is nice—"

"Your song is wonderful," said Papa,

"but the babies are asleep."

So Penny went to her room

and shut the door.

Penny started to sing,

"One is nice, two is nice,

three is even better . . ."

Penny stopped.

She wanted someone

to listen to her.

Penny sang to herself

in the mirror.

That didn't work.

Penny sang

to her glass animals.

That didn't work, either.

Penny made faces at herself
in the mirror.

Then she moved her glass animals
around on the top
of her dresser.

She almost forgot about her song.

Chapter 2

Soon it was time to eat.

"Listen, everyone," said Penny.

"It's my very own song."

Penny started to sing,

"One is nice, two is nice,

three is even better.

Four is nice—"

"Not at
the table,"
said Mama.

"After dinner,"
said Papa.

After dinner Penny sang

for Mama and Papa

and the babies.

This was Penny's song:

"One is nice, two is nice,

Three is even better.

Four is nice, five is nice,

Six in rain is wetter.

Seven is nice, eight is nice,

Nine is almost best.

But ten is even bigger,

And is better than the rest."

"That was beautiful!" said Mama.

"That was wonderful!" said Papa.

The babies made baby noises.

"Thank you," said Penny.

Penny sang her song again.

Then everyone sang Penny's song.

Mama sang high and softly.

Papa sang low and loudly.

Penny sang in the middle
and clearly.

Beautifully.

The babies sang
in their own baby way.

Then they did a little show.

Mama wore funny sunglasses.

Papa wore a silly hat.

Penny wore her feather boa.

The babies wore
what they were wearing.
They all sang and sang
and sang.

"I'm tired," said Mama.

She flopped onto a chair.

"I'm tired," said Papa.

He plopped onto the sofa.

The babies were tired.

They fell asleep

in their basket.

Mama laughed.

"At first I thought you would
wake up the babies," she said.

"And now," said Papa,
"you have helped them
fall asleep."

Penny yawned.

She was tired, too.

"We had a good time,"
  said Penny.

"Speaking of time," said Mama.

"Do you know what time it is now?"

"Time to sing it again?"
  said Penny.

"No," said Papa. "Time for bed."

Mama turned off
the light.

Papa picked up
the babies.

Penny led
the way upstairs.

Everyone kissed everyone.

"Will I remember my song
   in the morning?" asked Penny.

"Yes," said Mama.

"Are you sure?" asked Penny.

"Yes," said Papa.

And they were right.

Penny remembered her song.

Beautifully.